George Henry Calvert

Life, Death and other Poems

Volume 1

George Henry Calvert

Life, Death and other Poems
Volume 1

ISBN/EAN: 9783337403829

Printed in Europe, USA, Canada, Australia, Japan

Cover: Foto ©Andreas Hilbeck / pixelio.de

More available books at **www.hansebooks.com**

LIFE, DEATH,

AND

OTHER POEMS.

BY

GEORGE H. CALVERT.

BOSTON:
LEE AND SHEPARD, PUBLISHERS.
NEW YORK:
CHARLES T. DILLINGHAM.

The Riverside Press, Cambridge :
Electrotyped and Printed by H. O. Houghton & Co.

LIFE, DEATH,
AND OTHER POEMS.

CONTENTS.

———◆———

LIFE.

Life sparkles with poetic gleamings,
  As Heaven with lucent stars.
  Unto the deeper dreamings
Of the soul's solitude, fresh bars
  Of tenderest music bring
  A delicate nourishment,
As to our inmost virtue sing
Chorals, of angel voices blent.

The Powers that launch a human soul
  On life's eternity,
  On towards a boundless goal,
  Joy with creative glee,

Mid supersolar lights,

Mid unapproachable mights,

Whose will peoples th' infinitudes of space,

Whose playthings are wild comets' fiery race.

Children of light are we and truth,

Luminaries, to beam for aye

In an unwrinkled youth;

Untouched by sour decay,

When once we be uprisen

Above this earthen prison,

Loaded no more with flesh, erect and glad

We soar, buoyant and free, only with spirit clad,

Towards cleaner, wiser thought ever to mount,

Upbuoyed by Love, that streams,

From unimaginably holy fount,

Through all our doings, fancies, dreams,

Purging them of their stains
And red, impassioned pains,
In God's soft arms enfolded we :
This is our possible destiny.

Truth watches us with sleepless eye
From far, superimperial throne,
Set deeper in the glittering sky
Than the one constant star who all alone
Guides our dark courses on the sea, —
One of Truth's raptured servants he, —
While she, puissant in primal dower,
Sways the whole universe with God's unmeted power,

And hand in hand with her twin-sister, Love,
Together they enclasp the naked moth
And planets and the steadfast suns above,
And all that throbs, e'en to the froth

That rides a moment on the billow's back,
Illuming the dim caverns of remorse,
Lighting life ever on its shadowed track,
Missing no birth, and smiling on the birthful corse.

Th' invisible Heaven unresting weaves
Around, within us life's quick web
With threads finer, more beautiful than sheaves
Of light forth from her eyes by midnight shed.
And what a gift is human life!
To be a new immortal spirit!
Wooed by th' eternities, that it grow rife
The bliss and beauties of angelic good t' inherit.

Around, above, within us beat, —
Inaudible to earthen senses, —
Th' eternal pulses of creative heat
Aye wreathing spiritual recompenses,

For which, through holy fires that in us burn,
We with a sane forefeeling yearn,
We the choice children of all-folding Might:
Not compassed round with darkness are we, but with
light.

DEATH.

LIFE's loving brother, indefatigable Death,
    Keeps Life alert and young.
    Without him, Life's sweet breath,
Rank and unbreathable through healthy lung,
  Would sicken Life himself, that, pale
  As frighted sky in an eclipse,
  His eyes grow blear, his spirits fail,
  Smiles vanish from his leaden lips,
  And, shuddering in a dull despair,
  To see matter's unchecked increase,
  Would shriek towards Heaven a piteous prayer
    That he might quick decease,
Ere he be suffocated by

His offspring. They, up piled in monstrous mounds,—
    Now that they cannot die, —
No longer know or beauty, grace, or bounds ;
In unproportioned crowds of lurid life
    Pressing each other for more room,
    Wrangle in unavailing strife,
    Faith and Hope waning in the gloom
    Exuded from usurping matter ;
The watchful angel no more there to shatter
    Its tightening fetters, hopeless age
Wailing in swarms of slow decrepitude,
    Impotent to die, and thus elude
        The shocks of helpless rage
    At its imprisonment on earth, —
    Earth in soiled ragged gray enwrapt,
    Of its dear greenery unsapt,
    Grown to a gross material Hell,
    Where never more is heard the knell

Of a new liberating birth;
Boyhood outnumbering childhood, manhood both,
While age, more numerous than all the three,
    Gasps in imbecile sloth,
Cursing its heavenly privilege to be.

    Banish good Death, and all things soon
        In agony would pray
For his recall, to lift them out of swoon,
    To free them from deathless decay.
    Aye, Heaven's brave minister is he,
        The world's unwearied cleanser,
    Divine in his ubiquity,
Of freshness and of sweetness the dispenser,
    Unresting key that is forever
    Opening the bridal bloom of spring!
Triumphant spirit, that dost seem to sever
The body thou renew'st and dost re-wing.

Gross earthy thoughts have made the scythe
Thy symbol, with grim skeleton, and skull
Grinning in mockery of life.   A blithe
  Ethereal figure, beautiful
  As a May-dawn, or peeping pink
  Of the first rose, or maiden's blush,
  Or boreal joy's ecstatic flush, —
These were fit symbols for earth's beautifier,
  Man's lifter to th' angelic choir;
    For thou, thou art the link
Twixt life and life.   Dear Death! loud hail to
    thee!
Thou holy handmaid of eternity!

All nature keeps itself alive by dying, —
Seeming to die; bodies even die not,
They do but change; for spirit is ever plying
Creative power; and so from rankest rot

Of matter life upsprings,
Exulting in fresh wings,
Breathing with a new breath
Inbreathed from high beneficence: THERE IS NO DEATH.

SPRING.

Late art thou, but to come thou couldst not fail,
Divinest minister of the divine.
    Firstling of the great Sun, we hail
    Thy bounteous plenitude of green,
    Sprung from the deep mysterious mine
Of life, unfathomable and unseen.
Thou floodst our hearts with beauty from the bloom
      Of thy young, happy face,
      And from our thoughts their gloom
    With virgin joyousness dost chase,
    And tremulous glee of flowering trees,
With whose fresh beauties the caressing breeze
Dallies, showering sweet breath into the air,

2

And sunny kisses, with bold stealth
Seizing their vernal perfumes rare,
Enriching nature with her own new wealth.
This sudden sun-born burst
Of leafy life all round our earth,
Quick resurrection of hushed nature, hearsed
In winter's crypt, this bright rebirth,
This universal blossoming,
This certain strangling of cold death
By the warm Herculean breath
Of the reviving Spring
In her old earthen cradle, — this
Rhythmic renewal of deep nature's bliss,
Is token from th' all-loving and all-seeing
Of man's reblossom'd joy in a perennial being.

GARIBALDI.

AGAIN is Italy summoned to mourn,
　　Yet with a thankful cheerfulness,
　　That her loved Hero is upborne
　　When the high work,'t was his to bless
　　　　His country with, is done.
　　Distracted Italy is one,
　　United, self-directing, free
　　　　Of foreign force, while he,—
　　　　One of her saviors, who
As child could bravely save an adult life,
　　And, foremost of a patriot crew,
Spent a stout manhood in ennobling strife, —
　　Ascended to his burnished seat

Blest by full hearts, which he had swelled
  With freemen's blood and made to beat
   With pulses that had quelled
  Fierce tyrannies.   The famous man
Passed calmly on, more reverenced, more dear,
  To a new, thankful nation than
  Any son living.
       'Bove his bier
All the past greatness shone of Italy;
  All souls that through the struggling ages
Had boldly fostered her high destiny,
The men who live in consecrated pages,
Whom we that breathe outside the warm confines
   Of Alps and Apennines,
  Study for high enlightenment
  And stouter bracing of our souls, —
  Pages whence the new hardiment
  Of hero or of thinker rolls
  Upon us waves of strength and thought:

These gloried ones shine there in circles wrought
Of superearthly splendor, quick to greet,
  With heavenly salutation meet,
Their Garibaldi, him who, single-handed,
Had wrested from the tyrants 'gainst him banded
Populous Naples and broad Sicily,
And given them to triumphant Italy:
  Cavour, Mazzini, who so well
In his large soul foredrew the nation's span,
      Victor Emmanuel,
      The patriot King, and man
So true, that he deserved to be
King of emancipated Italy;
  Manin, and many others who
      With heart-beat strong and true,
  Had spent them for their country's good.
      To him these were the nearest,
      Yet hardly were they dearest,

So many had outpoured their blood
To enrich with freedom a lov'd land.
The aspiring Poets all were there.
Poets are patriots by command
Of love, warmed by the ideal glare
Which lights their being.   Alfieri the proud,
Who sang of liberty, with a stern pen
Straight'ning the souls of crouching countrymen,
To lone, sublimest Dante, whom the shroud
Of exile could not deaden, but he soared
On flashing pinion from Hell's lowest story,
Through thickly peopled Purgatory,
High up to saintly Beatrice the adored.
All came who with the glow of beauty
Illuminate their land through Art,
Or clasp her in the motherly arms of duty.
Savonarola took close part
Beside Da Vinci, Angelo, Raphael;

Heaven-widening Galileo hand in hand
    Hovered with Titian.   The strong spell
Of the new glory swelled the crowded band
    With great Antiquity, when Rome
    Was Europe.   Came from highest home
    The Brutuses and Cicero,
    Long clean of anger, pain, and woe,
    True Scipios and Antonines,
All glittered round Caprera's sea-set lines.
    With lightning looks of exultation,
    Outshining earth-drawn ecstasy, —
      Looks of emancipation, —
    Amid seraphic melody,
    Too piercing pure for mortal's ear,
    With glow, as of rainbows intermingled,
Great Garibaldi tenderly outsingled,
    Heavenward with jubilant joy they steer;
Him, now to immortal spirit-figure moulded,
They loving waft aloft in angel-arms enfolded.

ASPIRATION.

Th' innumerable Suns that star the vault
    We wonder in, when our own Sun
    Unrolls mysterious night, assault
The soul with such sublimities, they stun
    Our earthly thinkings.   When we strain
    Feeling and thought to seize their meanings,
        We vivify the brain
        With quick creative gleamings,
And these, speaking with voice of solar light,
    Unveil a supersolar Might.
        Man's *thought* can never grasp,
    But his high *feeling* can enclasp
    This Might.   With the spirit of the whole

Can swell and bound the soul,
For of infinitude we are,
And towards the farthest star
Can speed ourselves in happy awe,
Seize its eternal law,
And feed great yearnings.   We
Are parcel of eternity,
A portion of all that we feel and see;
Not th' outward world alone, but Deity
Mirrors itself upon the procreant brain,
That glowing centre of circumferences
Unlimited, where endless is our gain.
Spirit is never subject unto fences,
But with devout elation
Moves through the brightening brightness of creation.
Man can reflect this brightness
Because of the inward rightness
Of his deep nature.   He longs for the better;

His true nobility chafes at the fetter
    Of bondman, aiming to be freer,
On ever higher, purer, to uprear
    His being. And in his puissant self
Is the divinity that aye protests
'Gainst pressures that would lay him on the shelf
Of apathy, foiling his high behests.
He is a wingéd creature, his wings beating
    Invisibly the air, to lift him
    To higher ranges, thus defeating
    The lower; he aye longs to sift him
    Of gross carnalities, and mount
        Towards spirit's primal fount,
    Struggling to obey his soul's attraction
    From mouldy sloth to polished action,
    Inwardly mourning when dull vice
Embraces him in its constrictive ice.
At times, amid the passions devilish

Of a bad man, upshoots a holy wish,
Like infant's chirp within a robber's cave,
    That circumfuses all
    The father's heart, melting the pall
Of evil; or like a single star,—when rave
The tempest's demons,—that peeps through the
    storm's
Cold blackness, and the sailor's heart rewarms.
Life should be a curriculum of prizes :
Man is the more himself the more he rises:
'T is his angelic instinct to aspire :
Manhood must mount, from low to high, from high to
    higher.

TRUTH.

In the hale birth-throes of first being
Was born this God, this bold, all-seeing,
 All-beautifying Truth,
 This old, eternal Youth.
 A universal presence,
He rides upon the Sun's fierce beams,
He floats among the Sea's calm dreams;
His birthful breath makes nature's crescence.
A thousand stars glow in his eye;
Quintessence of divinity,
God calls him when he doth create;
He in creation hath no mate.
Without him man were less than beast,

And life a tasteless, hopeless feast.
Loosen Truth's hold on human thought,
Shadow his splendor in the feeling,
And, like a painted savage caught
By cruel potions, man goes reeling.

    In the broad brain Truth quires
    As lightning in the air,
When, leaping from his cloudy lair,
Stagnation he with motion fires.

    Man's quenchless guardian-light,
Truth pilots him through wreckful night,
And should he stumble into crime,
Uplifts him with a call sublime.

    Truth is man's spiritual Sun,
Older, more luminous, than the one
We walk by in Time's small periphery,
Our beaming monitor through all Eternity.

IDEAL.

In what a nest of love and joy,
    And holy mystery,
    He lay, the baby boy !
    Hope in her heavenliest glee
Hovering, and pouring from above
Sparkles into the eyes of joy and love.
    A soul-bud, beautiful
As angel's smile on the dawn beaming,
    Life, mighty life, astreaming
    Through him in currents full
Of perfumed promise, his soft breathing
To firmer beauty roseate limbs awreathing ;
For the great Sun looks on him lovingly,

Ripening the finer elements of air
To mould him to proportion's grace, while He
Who moulds the Sun, and hath creative care
     Of universal being,
Freights his new breath with subtle filaments
That speed, like lightning to our seeing,
To the brain, building with fire its vast contents,
     Sowing it with the seeds
     Of crownéd thoughts and deeds,
  Making it exquisitely rife
  With all the fragrancies of life.
  His daily living grows to be
  One long unbroken blossoming,
     And like some tropic tree,
     Unstung by frost's cold sting,
     In prodigal opulence
Outthrowing mingled sweet incense
Of flower and fruit from the same branch,

New, generous plans bloom near to staunch
Nutritious deeds.   But he is still a child
      Springing toward youth from station
To station, on the strong faith lifted
      Of fearless expectation;
      And ever undefiled,
For that young spirit is so gifted
      With human upward swing
      That in his brain is plied
Triumphantly Life's subtlest skill
In moulding individual will.
Pure as the thoughts of modest bride,
Or consciousness that good deeds bring,
      Are his desires.
      Like lofty spires
      Upstreaming in the sky
      From solid sure foundations,
They mount; not groveling in a sordid sty,

But in their swift mutations
Are so unselfed that angels hear them,
Taking delight to come down helpful near them.
The warm tempestuous straits
That palpitating youth sails through
He passed unscathed amid the baits
Of fragrant sensualities untrue,
Above his head unconsciously unfurled, —
Daunting th' hypocrisies of the world, —
The hallowed flag of innocence.
He entered manhood's strenuous path,
Invigorated by the intense
Clean strength of youth's elastic bath.
Fresh life he drew from a so fervent power,
It strengthened, sweetened, sanctified each hour.
Welcome as scented breeze
In spring, mysterious as the light
Of silent stars, resistless as decrees

3

Of Fate, and with the might
Of deepest heave of Ocean,
Cometh, flame-crested, the warm wave
Of love, flooding with rapturous emotion,
And with imaginings so bold and brave,
His being's core, that he feels recreated,
As with a larger soul dilated.
And now his life put on its earnestness.
The titles, husband, father, were a claim
His fellows had that he should bless
His household with th' ascending flame
Kindled by countrymen's and neighbor's prayer
For its victorious weal.
His manhood shone in thoughtful care
Of largest interests, such as deal
With the mind's loftiest life, and with
Sound enterprises, of such pith
They strengthen while they purge

The vital currents of communities.

　　His hopes, sprung from the purest deeps
Of intuition, bore him to the verge
　　Of present possibilities.
　　He stood upon the heights whence leaps
　　To loftier heights prophetic vision,
(The heights that gender popular derision.)
　　　　In these profoundest moods,
When on itself the mind creative broods,
He looked like Shelley, or still younger Keats,
When rapt, by inspiration inly stirred,
　　With head upturned, on magic seats
They hearken for the voice by genius heard;
　　For he, too, was a poet.　Verse
He wrote not, but that rhythmic sweep of thought
　　He had which comes of feelings wrought
　　By noble sympathies, that nurse
　　The will to lofty deeds, and send

The wishes outward where they blend
With beauty's magic to create
On the broad solid ground
Of practice just, compelling very Fate
To second his aspiring bound.
So rich he was in human feeling,
And on his lustrous path he trod
With such religious sure reliance
Ever to largest principles appealing,
That like great Kepler in celestial science,
He, too, could think the thoughts of God.
Unto the beautiful, — wherein
Creative mind is most revealed, —
His soul was so akin,
That to him were unsealed
Secrets of the vast All.
Much of its mystery
Was opened to him in the fall

Of Niagaras, in the tideful sea,
   In midnight orbs' wise twinkle,
 In the calm throb of his own pulse,
 In the auroral lights that sprinkle
   The night-born dew with glory,
 In the great thunders that convulse
The clouds, in all the heroic traits of Story.
   Nay, in the common and the little
    Flashes the beautiful,
 In grass and grain, in every tittle
Of visible, audible nature, in the dull
   As in the bright. Creative power
Is nowhere felt but there upflames the dower
   Of beauty's life. The microscope
   Reveals the beautiful in mud,
Flaring upon us an immense new hope,
For tiniest earthy particle is a bud
Of promise. What, — could its keen focus reach
Into the darkest heart, — what would it teach?

Men, living men, were his rich source
Of knowledge ; for in them the fineness
 Outshone, beside the force,
 Of infinite divineness.
His daily comrades were the great
Of the big past, men of such weight
 Their fiery thoughts and deeds
 Become prolific seeds
Planted in the universal mind.
The mightiest of men, the Nazarene,
 The topmost man of all his kind,
 Whose life was in the clean
Inspiring deeps of sympathy,
Him he aye studied as an exemplar
 Of the highest in humanity.
 Thinking good thoughts, looking afar
 Beyond the smaller self,
The worldly lusts of show and power and pelf,

His day lighted by loves, ne'er dimmed by fears,
 He grew in wisdom with the years,
His life one limpid stream of joyous duty,
 Which filled it full as June with beauty,
 So full that time brought him no oldness.
Spirit ruled him as it ruled Socrates;
And so, when on his flesh at last crept coldness,
Shone bright before his spiritual eye the keys
Of th' Heav'n he had made about him on the earth;
 And from his body's bier
He rose in th' ecstasy of a new birth,
His face aglow with beams thrown from th' angelic
 sphere.

REAL.

O FOR a pen whose ropy ink
    Were purged by piteous tears!
    So when I come to think
Of th' omnipresent ill that sears
The tender, sapful, noble human heart,
Words may grow tremulous with fellow-pain,
    But bold to take the part
    E'en of the lowest, who have lain
    Wallowing in crime and lust.
Can we be loyal to our higher being,
    Can we be pious, loving, just,
    Our inward eyes open to seeing
    What went before and is to come, —
    Our love and pity will grow deeper,

But so with hope enlightened, that the dumb
Would speak to us, and smile the very leper.
In what a hot-bed of uncleanness, want,
>> And gross publicity,
>> That mother, famished, gaunt,
Gives birth to him who is to be
>> A man 'mong other men!
The first breath that babe breathes is foul,
His cradle is a crowded pen
Of blighted manhood, whence a ghoul
Would fly, baffled by bloodless pallor,
>> Where unseen devils grin
In mockery of human squalor
>> And misery's plaintive din.
>> In such an atmosphere,
>> In a slim stalk so rooted,
None of the juices can inhere
>> Of blooming babyhood.

The mother's milk that makes his blood
With oozy slime is sooted,
No blossoms sprout, but only thorns,
And these turn tortuous back upon their stem,
Poisoning its tardy sap.   Upon his morns
Nor joy nor sunbeams shine, to sweeten them.
Begotten so, so bred,
The sportful fairies, whose delight
It is to play among the curls
Of dimpled childhood's head,
Sprinkle upon him tiny pearls
Of tears, and saddened take their flight.
Missing th' ambrosial endless bath
Of feminine tenderness, that hath
Quick nurture in it for his craving heart, ˜
He languishes and droops.
Hardly hath he a childhood in these coops
Of deprivation, suffering aye the smart

Of pain, he whose whole day should be
Joyous as morning's sunlit dew,
Painless as a young air-fed tree,
Thankful as April's carol new.
Nature, with her close lessons, was to him
Less than a step-dame.   In her lenient lap
'T was not for him to lie : he was a limb
Torn from her cruelly, which her sweet sap
Could no more animate ; for e'en her fount
  Within him was befouled by rank
   Bitter and weedy juices.
   The flood from feeling's sluices
  Ran inward ; he became a tank
Secluded, sunless, whence could mount
No breathing to the God of Right.

Was due his soured maiméd plight
To antenatal deprivation.

Not guilty was he of self-desecration:
　　His birth-gifts were lesions and losses;
　　Nature herself, she shut him off
From Nature; for her boons he had her crosses;
A nightmare dim, was life, he could not doff;
The goads that pricked him to a guilty tomb
　　She fastened on him in the womb.
He was born chained, nor could he wish him free;
Growing into false freedom he became
A Bedouin of the street; he could not be
　　Forecasting worker; a good name
　　He never could be crowned with; Crime
　　　　Crouching about him, spread
　　　　Its pliant net, which Time
　　　　Tightened about his head.

What is man — what, society —
And what is Nature's self, that she

Should mock us with such fellows, men
Who issue not from homes, but from a den,
To prey upon their brothers; for they are
Our brothers, seared at birth with sin's black scar,
 Souls damned ere they have lived their life,
Their life a doom of hate and bleeding strife.
Why live they, these curst creatures, men who dare
No whither look; if inward, they are met
 With the soul's shudder; if they glare
At Heaven, the stars twinkle a threat.

  Mysterious being sweeps
From height to height, from deep to deeps,
  Higher and deeper ever;
  And man's upright endeavor
Can compass more and more these heights,
  The more his own deep being
  Grows master of the mights
Wherewith his soul is gifted by the all-seeing.

Himself partakes of the creative power:
This is his bounteous mighty dower.
Such mastery is a token
Of manhood, strong to have broken
Many a chain that bound him,
And with Truth's diadem becrowned him.
Within him are the forces that uplift
His life to this free altitude.
Such freedom is a gift
With spiritual sovereignty endued.
He is become more than an earthly king,
And rules, as Jesus rules,
Through indestructible rights which bring
Resistless sway, that schools
Men's minds through their own light
Kindled by the supremest might.
In this exalted zeal
Angels become his aids, for they

Are only men who think and feel
More finely, having dropped their clogging clay.

When through a self-earned moral sovereignty
Many shall have become loyal and free,
Then these can free their brothers, 'bolish jails,
 Silence the multitudinous wails
 Of vice and crime. But we are all
As yet too heedless of the higher call,
Too much the slaves of sense and fallacies.
We build luxurious jails, and call them palaces;
Out of the common self and vain conceits
We build theologies that cannot save,
Being but rotting steps, showy deceits,
 That wilder and the more enslave.
This self-emancipation is a weary
 Unceasing battle of the higher
Against the lower self, often with dreary

Outlook; but God is not a liar,
Who gave us reason, hope, and aspiration
    That they should droop unto prostration.
Onward and upward is the rally-cry
    That ever sounds above the din
Of life's tough war, aye, cheering us to die
    Champions of freedom from sour sin.
Deep in the best souls lives a true ideal,
And interlinked therewith, as love with duty,
    Forever glows the consciousness
That we ourselves and brother men can bless
    With daily and supremest beauty,
        Marrying th' ideal with the real.

THE BEAUTIFUL.

I.

THROUGHOUT th' eternal sequences of time
Momently is shed by every fiery Sun
Of the hot hundred millions safely spun
Into immensity by the sublime
Almighty Will, the Beautiful, whose clime
Is the universal air, across which run
Ceaseless creative messages that stun
Our thought, straining after words to rhyme
With th' unimaginably great.   In each
Creative thought glows, as its very soul,
The Beautiful, which is essence divinest,
That colors, shapes and perfumes the vast Whole
And every part, e'en to the simple finest,
Sparkling wherever thought and feeling reach.

4

THE BEAUTIFUL.

II.

BEAUTY'S deep office holy is to teach,
Through the purification of delight
Kindling into clear vision the higher sight.
Within a cove, upon a sunny beach,
I have seen the mighty Ocean,— without breach
Of his high privileges, stormful might
Laying aside,— come calmly in, with bright
Dear children, round, ruddy, as ripened peach,
To toy, gently rolling low-crested billows
Into their fearless arms,— like monarch playing
On the floor with his gleeful boys, arraying
Himself in love instead of robe and crown,—
The waves wooing the little limbs like pillows:
A sight the eyes in lustral tears to drown.

ROSA.

She was a child, and not a child,
　　She looked so blandly wise
　　Out of her large blue eyes.
　　Her gentleness was wild
　　With a quick freedom fawn-like,
　　And freshness that was dawn-like.
　　Docile to all her teaching,
Yet from within she seemed to draw
The best, and, as she were upreaching
For something that she heard or saw,
　　Would silent sit, her head
Upturned in visionary mood,
As though her tender thoughts were fed

By angels with unearthly food.

Two romping brothers, who were older,

At first would rudely mock her

For trances that did hold her

Apart.   But soon they ceased to shock her

With boyish gibings.   She

By sure degrees became

To them a mystery

For which they had no taunting name.

The father's love almost to awe

Was lifted towards his blooming girl,

Who with deep tenderness could thaw

His colder moods, as she would coy unfurl

Before him thoughts so luminously true

They soothed with lessons holier than he knew.

Lovelier she blossomed with each year,

As though creative spirit rained its best

Upon her, and would rear

A being ablaze with Beauty's sovereign crest,
   Beauty, sovereign solely through glow
      Of clean unselfish feeling;
And then it is the promise-bended bow
      A heaven above revealing.
   Her father and her brothers felt, —
      And half unconsciously, —
This subtle power, that could melt
      To tenderness the three,
      And on her bearing throws
      Its grace, as on the rose
A fragrant sap the rose's loveliness.
   Upon the mother's heartstrings press
      Close sympathies so deep
      They her whole nature tune
      To harmonies that steep
Her in a faith that nothing can impugn.
      Every hour she would fold
      The daughter to a breast,

That almost ached with love it could not hold,
Thus easing a sweet fulness that oppressed.
Rosa would lie in infinite content,
    Their beings each in other blent.

    At noon one day she was not there;
    Empty at dinner, too, her place.
    Then they all learnt what a cold air
    They breathed without her glowing face.
    And still she came not: then grew pale
    The mother, restless the two brothers.
        The father, with a male
Paternal strength comforting the lone mother's
    Quick fears, strode into the small town,
        The boys following in tears.
        Soon, loosened from all fears,
        They were upon her track;
For she already had a dear renown

For beauty and for kindliness.   Ran back
    The joyful, weeping, elder brother
    To bring joy to his weeping mother.
They found her in a fever-stricken hovel,
    With soft wet cloths cooling the skin
    Of two young children.   They who grovel
In the abjectness of vain self-pampering
    Would start at that which Cherubin
    Are holier for witnessing. —
Beside them, on another bed of straw,
    Their mother lay, her features lank
With the worn pallor which gaunt fevers gnaw.
      When Rosa moved to follow,
    She scarcely had the strength to thank
Her gentle nurse.   When Rosa kissed her hollow,
    Wan cheek, she reverently laid
    Her hand upon the child, and said,
      "O come, O come again!"

Her words thrilling with thankfulness and pain.
The body goes, the soul remains.
When Rosa passed into the street
Her presence still was felt, nor could the pains
Resume their wasting heat.
A soul-joy planted near a sorrow
Works with such healing sympathy
That even by to-morrow
The grief will no more be.
The soul is a creative power :
It builds this wondrous fleshly frame,
And it can cure the ills that cower
Within it, life to lame.
Souls are all brothers, and the healthiest
Draws from its primal source
A deep benignant force,
To which the first and wealthiest
Of earthly goods is empty chaff

Winnowed by wind from wheat,
Or as the worldling's laugh
Wherewith he would his own soul cheat.
Rosa ran on, before her father, brother,
To meet her dearest mother.

In a gifted girl, outringing
Joy in a healthy home, a fervor,
Of life is ever bringing
Fresh will and strength to nerve her
For each return of morning. Sorrow
As yet could take no living root,
But each day's little grief the morrow
Dried off ere it could grow to fruit.
Rosa, with all her inward brooding,
Was most herself when other eyes
Looked into hers. She, excluding
None from her love, closely could prize

Both old and young, the false and true man :
　　Herself so fully human.
Where the rays fell of her warm eyes
They made love sprout, in her school-mates
Growing so strong, it crushed the lies
　　Of Envy, which abates
Rarely its rancor towards the gifted good :
Envy feeds on its own infected blood.
　　So alive was she with fellow-feeling,
　　Her ruling impulse was to help
　　　　The weak, happiest when kneeling
　　By the sick poor ; nor was the whelp
　　Of heartless lust beyond the reach
　　Of her capacity to teach.
A sympathetic tenderness can waken
A hope, a love, in soul the most forsaken.
　　　　Angelic instincts taught her
There is a soul of good in evil things.

And now caressing years had brought her
A fifteenth May, when life its censer swings
    With freshest perfumes laden.
Never did flowers enrich their bloom
    With joy of heavenlier maiden;
    For in and through this glow, —
As light upon a landscape's beauty,
Transfiguring the outward show, —
Shone the pure soul of love and duty,
Which, like th' invisible spirit that makes
    Night's starr'd sublimity,
In the beholder's raptured being wakes
    Feelings of high divinity.
    Athrough the portals garlanded
      Of womanhood she gazed
    With feelings less with sadness sped
    Than joy; nor was the vista hazed
    With passion's dim imaginings,

Which make the self an ever-shifting centre
   Of prosperous being. Wings,
Gilded by whiter rays, young Fancy lent her,
  Rays that illume a higher plane
   Whereon both joy and pain
   Are tempered by emotion
   That stills the soul's high yearning,
  Like cordial piety's devotion
  Invisible inward incense burning.
Beyond the self she could untimely look,
   Having as child far visions,
Wiser than those that from a darkened nook
Rule th' aged worldling's confident decisions.
   Appearances had never flattered
   Even her untilled youth
  With misty magnifyings. Truth
   Enveloped her and shattered
The films that cause the false and small to seem

The large and true, and make,
To most, life a delusive dream,
From which on earth they never wake.
So, into womanhood she carried
Infantile innocence, with its first tender
Blossoms, indissolubly married
With angel's wisdom to defend her.
Her life she could not live amid the shoals
And sands whereon life's ocean rolls,
And breaks its mightiness in foam.
Like the finned travelers of the sea,
Her sole congenial home
Was in the deeps, of deep humanity.
And these she found beside
The shoals; for always there are deeps
Where is a soul; and where abide
Its master-loves, and leaps
Its inmost flame, she peered,

And met thankful reflection of her feeling,
    Thankfullest from hearts most seared.
    Like Pharos high she stood, appealing
        To passers mid false Fashion's
    Cold shallows and unfervent passions.
    None were repelled.   Her beauty drew
    All to her, as the magnet steel,
And then, her modest earnestness but few,
Nay none, could long withstand, and they would feel
        Their hearts warm with new love.
        A jealous matron spoke
    To Rosa with a sneer would move
A worldly girl's quick wrath; it could provoke
    In her only meek humbleness.
" Nay, I pretend to naught," with a deep blush
    She said, that made her loveliness
        So whelming, it could crush
The matron's jealousy, that she, with look

Of mingled love and shame,
　　The dazzling maiden took
Into her arms, — with a self-blame
　　Not known before, — did press,
And with true tenderness caress.
Upon her cheek Rosa's tears fell
　　As Heaven's gift of rain
In autumn to depleted well.

Into that glowing focus, Rosa's brain,
　　　　Had poured their ripening rays
　　　　Twenty-one summers; she
Felt the high part that woman plays,
As yet but half self-consciously.
The mastering passion, that unveils
Life's beauties, wants, vibrations, deeps, —
As morning's glow earth's wonders, — assails
The whole strong being to wake from sleeps

That hold it passive, she had felt,
Not yielded to : she would not break
Her nature's wholeness, and she dwelt
In motives so impersonal, that, to stake
Them on uneven marriage, were
To risk her life's success.
The man, for whom she might have joyed
In love's full rapture, was both fair
To look on and to listen to ; to bless
Life-union too alloyed
With self. She lived out of herself, and he
For and within himself. Her mate
She knew he could not be ;
She knew, moreover, how to school her.
So strong she was and pure, she made the Fate
Herself, that seemed to rule her.
The heights whereon she lived were heights
From lowliness. Into the nights

Of bodily and spiritual need
She brought beams of th' illumination
That had so splendently enfreed
Herself.   There was accumulation
Of wealthiest wealth.   All that she owned
She would impart; and as her riches
Were boundless spiritual treasures, they were loaned
Freely as air or promises of witches.
In her, life was an ever active love.

As whitened Alps the Sun
With heavenly heat doth move
To pour unstinted streams upon
The thankful plains and valleys,
The warmth of her large soul
Drove her towards unprovided alleys,
To allay a ceaseless dole.
The freedom she enjoyed,
Through soaring powers inborn, —

5

By thoughtful will whetted, upbuoyed, —
Inspired her soul with life the thorn
 Of baffled love, that wounded
A tender bosom, to draw out,
To hush the petty cries that sounded
Through that wide palace, and to rout
The whimpering imps who would usurp
Its glowing hospitable halls.
  Thus did great Freedom, — greater
  Than passion-swayed Jupiter, —
  Offspring of spiritual will,
The roots of amorous love extirp,
  With its loud partial calls.
  Nay more, she could distill,
  From thwarted feeling, balm
  That opened wider view,
  And wrought that spirit-calm
Of conquest which doth aye renew

With freshened force the sway
Of the high self, and makes an atmosphere
For longer sight and action's surer way.
Thus of herself she grew more fully master,
    Turning to light whereby to steer
        What seemed at first disaster.

Life deepened round her, and the more she knew
        The more she found to do.
    Life deepened, but it darkened not.
    Seen deeper, life is nowhere dark.
    In lookers' vision is a spot
    That swallows up life's hopeful spark,
    A spot black with the inground grime
    Of false theologies and crime
    Ubiquitous.   Rosa saw deeper.
    Deeper she saw, because she felt
So deeply, purely.   Calm as dreamless sleeper,
    She saw the basest.

Near her dwelt
A cruel father of motherless daughters.
To them she came to be like a new mother
As naturally as waters
Their level find.   No other
Could have so long that door
Kept open.   Hospitality
He knew not, and his core
Was so unsocial that, to flee
A stranger's face and talk
No blandishment could balk.
Deeper than blandishment
Was Rosa's undesigned attractiveness.
In her triumphantly were blent
The soul's and body's best address.
He even loved to see her enter,
And by her tuneful voice
And the quick power her soulful manners lent her

His rudeness was entranced, as by a choice
      Adagio is wild leopard's.
      To his mild orphan girls
Her presence was a guardianship, as shepherd's
    To helpless flock.   To sudden whirls
Of wrathful ruggedness he was a prey,
    'Fore which, as galliots in a squall,
    His gentle daughters quailed.   One day,
      On provocation small,
  Or none, he thundered angry speech.
  Rosa rose quick with features flushed,
  Spoke warm rebuke at such a breach,
    And left the chamber.   Hushed
  As funeral group, the stillness broken
    By sobs, was that sad room.
  The father paced, pale, no word spoken ;
    The daughters sunk in gloom
At the thought, they should not see her more.

A slow half hour had gone : the door
Opened, and as the day's first light
On anxious crew, near rockbound coast,
Fighting 'gainst wind and night,
Broke on them Rosa's beaming face : almost
Shrieked the daughters.   Her countenance
Alight with spiritual beauty's fire, —
As one in heaven-transported trance
Listening to angelic quire, —
She approached the father, saying,
In voice atremble with humility, —
As were the soul's choice sparkle through it raying, —
"Pardon, O pardon me!"
Astounded, mute, he gazed;
Then humbly turning to his daughters mazed,
As he a life-wrong would confess
In tones of a strange tenderness,
He cried, "Forgive! forgive! forgive!"

Then noiseless left the room.
This is, to live, to live,
Inly said Rosa, as she felt the doom
Of tyranny was lifted.   Their warm tears
Of a new joy mingled with hers
In close embrace, hers who had plucked the burs
That daily pricked their hearts with monstrous fears.
Rosa had sweetened a whole family's breath,
Had planted life where had been death.

Aye, humanly to live
Is not, to keep alert
The senses with befitting food;
Is not, to make the corporal sieve, —
Which is but animated dirt, —
The end, it being a means to spiritual good;
Is not, to flatter passion
With wasteful repetition
Of its subservient ration,

To help hungry ambition
Up to its slippery heights,
To gather fruit that feeds
To plethora the greeds; —
But 't is, to work so that the soul
Be ever splendent with the lights,
The consecrated lights, of love and duty,
Illumination that from pole to pole
Keeps the earth freshened with unearthly beauty.
To arrest a tear before it fall,
And make it glisten in a smile,
To antidote a sore heart's gall,
Efface with truth incipient guile,
Divert a threatening hate,
And harness it to draw with love,
And thus to substitute for Fate
A lordlier mandate from above;
This is to brighten, vivify
Dear life, and lift it human high.

FOUNDATIONS.

LIKE the two hands that knead our daily bread,
Nature and man should work with even will
And watchfulness, when innocent childhood lifts
Its helpless palms and prayerful eyes, and prays
For love and wisdom in the guardianship
Of its young years.   Nature is ever wise,
Watchful and active as th' unhalting Sun,
That warms and keeps alive all earthly being.
On man Nature outpours her choicest wealth ;
He is entrusted to her motherly love ;
Part of herself, and yet, greater than she,
Reflectively creative, he doth rise
Out of great Nature, and above her soars ;

For he hath wings of thought, precursive thought,
Wherewith, and manful will, he rules his own
And her resources vast.

                  Hale human babe
Is a potential deity on earth ;
Lord of the outward world, if he do grow
To be lord of himself.   Deep Nature calls
On deeper man to mould an infant's powers
And inborn potencies, within man's sphere,
His boundless sphere, almost omnipotent.
Love and high reason are his master-gifts,
Empowering him to be like to a God.
Teach the loved child to know and love all things,—
Earthworms, that so beneficently work
Beneath the surface of the teemful soil,
Insects that buzz joyously through the air,
The bird who pipes a jubilant holiday
To tune man's heart into blithe harmony

With this all-quickening multitudinous life,
The obedient horse and ox that multiply
His strength a hundred-fold.   Show him the Sun
Setting dim dawn ablaze with full-orbed light,
Higher and higher in benignant power
Mounting to bounteous hot magnificence.
Teach him no fear; the rageful hurricane,
The thunderclap, let him not dread.   Teach him
To shrink before rebuke,— even though it be
No louder than the faintest whisper's breath,—
That from his deepest sounds with sacred voice.
Within his inmost is a deathless spark,
Of fire to guide and rule.   This is for him
The holy of holies.   Here, in humble awe,
Let him oft hearken: thus hearkening, he
Is nearest to th' Almighty.   When the stars
Look down on him, and he on them, is wrought
The chain that binds him to the supreme Mind:

These myriad eyes embrace him with their beams.
Like diamond, filling its quick heart with light
From the far sun, to glow with mingled fire,
Man's deep capacity for reverence
Swells to religious thought when midnight opes,
With shining stellar keys, Infinitude,
Deepening the moral beauty of his life.

POETRY.

Iᴛ is not in the trees or in the ocean,
Nor in the air or earth or spacious skies,
Nor in the forms of nature, or the motion
Of stream or fawn, not even in the eyes
Of woman: in the soul of man it lies,
This peerless, heavenly gift, creative power
That lights and consecrates all these, and plies
For man's uplifting in bright happiest hour
This dearest privilege and his divinest dower.

CEASELESS CREATION.

THE smile in the eye
Is born but to die.
The bud of the rose
Full blooms but to fade,
The faster it grows
The sooner 't is dead.
The mother's delight
At day-break is born,
'T is dead ere the night
Of the next gloomy morn:
The father, he strains
Through turmoil and strife;
Mid bafflings and pains

Death swallows his life.
Life 's all a dream,
Death is a sleep,
And joy but a gleam,
While trouble we keep.

Put out the great light
Of faith and of hope, —
In the darkness of night
You ever will grope ;
For hope and dear faith
Are the sun of the soul :
'T is your blindness that saith
All is dark, — like the mole.

The smile in the eye,
It never can die ;
From the soul 't is a flash

That in joy will survive
The gloom and the crash
Of this earthly hive.
A soul hath the rose
That renews its bright birth :
Perennial it blows
To sweeten the earth.
As star lost in day,
The babe hath been won
By glory of ray
Outshining the sun.
The mother's blind eyes
Can't see its ascent,
As with saddest sighs
Her bosom is rent.
The babe comes down to her,
With kisses doth woo her,
With tenderest greeting

Whispers heavenly meeting.
The father, he meets it
(With a new sight he's blest),
In wonderment greets it,
From earth-toils at rest.

Life's not a mere dreaming,
'T is rather a beaming
From million-fold fire,
Each kindled and signed
By the infinite Mind,
Each aye straining higher.
Creative is life,
A ceaseless creation,
A getting things rife
For endless mutation.
For change is its law
And motion its joyance;

6

Its flow hath no flaw,
And it lives upon buoyance.
When once 't is in being
It never can cease ;
Delight of th' Allseeing,
Eternal its lease.

SKETCHES.

BETWEEN curved eyebrows and her auburn hair
  A smooth white forehead shone,
Like finest Parian glistening in the glare
Of genius' handwork, as, all alone
In beauty, flash the Paphian's wondrous limbs.
  The silken eyebrows arch above
   Soft eyes aglow with love,
  So warm, their lustre it bedims.
  A Cupid's bow are her two lips,
  So sweet, each of the other sips
  Moisture to make itself the sweeter.
In cheek and dimpled chin, small oval ear,
  Is nothing to defeat her
Dazzling, quick-conquering charm. A leer

Quailed before all this beauty, which
    Rounded her neck, then slid
    Lower, so fresh and rich
    Itself it quickly hid
(Like virtue from a wicked world
Or fear before a flag unfurled)
'Neath kerchief, laces and like covers,
Delicate provocatives to lovers.
But for this hiding, the far-famed
Greek Helen's bosom had been shamed.

These beauties *are* beauties, and great;
But they are for joyance, not sorrow,
For early years, not for the late,
For to-day, and not for to-morrow;
They are shallow, they cannot be deep,
Beauties when you can laugh, not when you weep.
    They wither too soon and grow cold,
    And die before they are old.

While admiration of a manly nose
>> And eyes cerulean blue,
O'erhung by eyebrows lightly brown,
Mounts towards climax on th' ivory hue
Of forehead with smooth wavy crown,
>> And in its rapture knows
Not where to pause, — all features melt
>> In a transfiguring light,
>> Which, like the sacred belt
Of halo, quickens blessèd sight.
From deathless inward beauty sprang
>> That belt of holy brightness,
Beauty of feelings, thoughts, that rang
With echoes from the soul of rightness.
Mere outward human beauty is a mask,
>> An empty, perishable cask.
>> Because within his brain are born
>> Powers angelic, given to bloom

In spheres higher than this, his earthly morn,
Man's compact countenance has the room
For supreme beauty, variousness and life.
Before a face and head thus nobly bright
Joyed admiration rose to fullest height,
Beholding great humanity so rife.

     Th' unconscious holder of such gifts
     And beauties rapturously gazed
     Upon the loveliness that blazed
        Beneath that auburn hair.
     'T was not the beauty that uplifts,
     Fresh as it was and rapturing fair.
He looked and passed; for him here was no mate.
Corporeal loveliness was not his bait.
A life-partner waited his coming, splendid
     From glow of feminine beauty blended
        Of purest innocence
     And rich emotion's reach, with sense
        So broadly masculine,

It lay beneath her feeling's nobleness
Like whitest marble of an Apennine,
Which Angelo's sure hand is to caress,
Beneath the fervent opulence and grace
Of flower and foliage on great Italy's fair face.

NO END.

THERE is no end: Eternity
Seizes each atom, and to be
    Involves unceasing growth.
      MIND quickens all:
    To die were rotting sloth,
Hateful impossible impotence.
Life tendeth upward, and to fall
    Is but a seeming, whence
    Uprise again all things:
Mind, their great mother, lendeth wings.
Heart-beats cease not within the tomb:
The " spiritual body " quits dissolving flesh,
    And far above a fleshly doom

Carries the soul's unceasing throb to fresh
    And higher planes of being.
    Life, in its million shapes,
    Is an incessant fleeing
From outworn moulds to new; escapes
    From matter's bonds, ascending
    Through infinite degrees,
Creating and effacing, rending
    Material forms with th' ease
    Of spirit-mastership,
    Aye razing to rebuild,
Through instantaneous power to equip
With its deep inwardness all atoms, filled
    Thereby with an instinctive need
    Of nursing every seed
Planted by overruling Mind.
    Mysterious Mind lends eyes
To all things, even to what seems blind,
To comets in the boundless skies,

Nor less to molecules that creep
Through th' universe, upbuilding it,
Mightiest of instruments, that heap
> Life upon life, and fit
Parts to their place in grandest wholes,
Obedient to primordial Will.
Mind launches thus infinitude of souls,
The purposes of being to fulfill,
Mind's mighty power and splendor aye attended
By thoughts of perfectness, so interblended
> With mind's own essence, that they glow
> Twin sovereign lights, — perennial bow
> Of promise, over all supreme.
> Immeasurably bright and pure,
They waken in all creatures soaring dream,
> And thereby all forever lure
> Upward towards better, higher,
Inflaming all with quenchless, holy fire.

OMNIPRESENCE OF BEAUTY.

BEAUTY is so deep 't is one with life,
And no imaginative knife
Can part their threads, close intertwined
By primal generative Mind.
Nay, Beauty might be called the life of being,
    Primordial essence bright,
  Aye, very soul of the all-decreeing,
Original, creative, holy Might. —
  Sea-shells come up from the salt sea,
  Sprinkling fresh beauty through their eyes,
  Iridescent interfusedly ;
    With gleam of sea-dipped dyes,
  And th' infinite grace of varying curves,

Refining, soothing tenderest nerves.
With what delight of recognition
We greet the peeping leaf-buds green,
  Into life's first fruition
Bursting in multitudinous sheen,
  With unslaked thirstiness
  Drinking the sweetened air,
Reveling in the sun's warm caress,
Outgushed so numerous, broad, and fair,
They make the forest's grandeur vast.
And now they are past, fallen, gone to enrich the roots
That nourished them.   But Beauty is not past.
  Instead of leaves, from each tree shoots
  Radiance, as though the sun
Had showered stars among the branches:
But for an hour; at noon are none,—
Melted by the same might that launches,
Even in winter, heated arrows. Lo!
  In a night Beauty re-assumes

His sway, sheeting with snow
Each twig and limb : the forest looms,
In the calm morning light,
A wondrous maze of sparkling white.
Again the sap reflows, and floods
The earth with leafy green.
A twofold beauty is in the woods,
A vocal rivaling the seen !
Music of a transcendant quire,
Cadence unreached by instrument or words,
Sweet improvisation, straining higher,
In the melodious worshiping of birds
At dawn, spontaneous anthem, rich and pure,
Mounting to Heaven whence it came,
To man's devotion timely overture,
Waking religious joy without a name.
From rivulet to river,
From cataract to dew,
From lakelet's shore to ocean's,

OMNIPRESENCE OF BEAUTY.

Great Beauty is the giver
Of joyance ever new :
Through aspects and through motions,
In Nature's colors, forms
Of leopard and of fishes.
In sunny calms, in storms,
In human thoughts and wishes,
In lightning's livid flashes,
In children's silken hair,
In eyes and soft eyelashes. —
Beauty is everywhere.
And man, if he himself must see it :
Chief child of Beauty, he should rise
To the height of his high birth : nay, he must be it
In feeling thought, if he would prize
The grandeur of his opportunities,
The splendor of his possibilities.
Beauty sparkles over surfaces because
It vivifies the core.

Inseparable from life, one are their laws :
    Beauty is the gold in life's ore.
        The highest we can know
        Is human life ; in man
        Beauty's great lessons glow
        Their deepest, in the van
        Of all corporeal being.
        His body, what a wonder !
Earth's supreme beauty, all o'erseeing,
Majestic more than any creature under
    Heaven's cope ; superlatively framed
        For strength, and spring, and grace,
Alone erect, by heat or cold untamed,
In his compact, far-looking, listening face
    Form and expressiveness unmatched.
    Behind upreaching forehead bold, —
    As Heaven's best will had been unlatched,
    And let loose potencies untold, —
That mighty product lies, the human brain,

The miracle of miracles, the seat
Of Mind; Mind which, once growing, never wanes,
But action follows its eternal beat.
 Mind! Through those sun-shaped orbs, the eyes,
  Lightens this mightiness!
 Behind in awful silence lies
 The tool of puissance only less
  Than high omnipotence, —
  Puissance of such a might
That should it rend its ordained continents
 Before its glare would pale all light
 Of suns, and to a whisper sink
  The tropic thunderburst.
  But on this fearful brink
We stand safe and assured. We are not curst
  By primal power: we are blest
 By a divine beneficence,
Potent to subject all to law's behest,
Wielding 'gainst chaos absolute defense.

And this quick instrument of soul,
This master-mass of matter superfine,
This vivid brain, is only great as whole
Through self-subsistent parts that all combine
    In rhythmical subordination,
Its maker, Mind, with the lower organs holding
    The infinite details of creation,
    With the highest in its grasp enfolding
    The largest, deepest, thought and feeling,
    The grandeur and the reach of Man,
His splendent possibilities revealing,
Therewith divinist beauty, purpose, plan.
    The nearer we to spiritual sources,
    The fuller, subtler, is the unfolding
Of Beauty's life. Man with his earthly forces
    Gets only glimpses bright, beholding,
Through deep, inspiring sensibilities,
      Resplendent tokens, signs,

Of what the supreme wisdom is

In its beneficent designs.

On earth man could easier the sun outstare

Than front, unblasted, Beauty's heavenliest glare.

www.ingramcontent.com/pod-product-compliance
Lightning Source LLC
Chambersburg PA
CBHW032203010726
47493CB00008BA/2799